Five reasons why you'll love Mirabelle . . .

Mirabelle is magical and mischievous!

Mirabelle is half witch, half fairy, and totally naughty!

She loves making potions with her travelling potion kit!

Mirabelle loves sprinkling a sparkle of mischief wherever she goes!

She has a little baby dragon called Violet!

If you had a baby dragon what would you call it?

My name! Eithne, and it means little fire!
—Eithne

Susan
—Callie

Fluffy Fireball
—Esther

Inferno
—Ava

Starblaze
—Tosia

Nogard—it's dragon
backwards!
—Hannah

Glitterwing
—Shihan

Family Tree

My mum
Seraphina Starspell

My brother
Wilbur Starspell

My dad
Alvin Starspell

Me!
Mirabelle Starspell

Violet

Illustrated by Mike Love, based on original artwork by Harriet Muncaster

OXFORD
UNIVERSITY PRESS

Great Clarendon Street, Oxford OX2 6DP
Oxford University Press is a department of the University of Oxford.
It furthers the University's objective of excellence in research, scholarship, and education by publishing worldwide. Oxford is a registered trade mark of Oxford University Press in the UK and in certain other countries

First published in 2024

British Library Cataloguing in Publication Data

Data available

ISBN: 978-0-19-278798-9

1 3 5 7 9 10 8 6 4 2

Printed in China

Paper used in the production of this book is a natural, recyclable product made from wood grown in sustainable forests. The manufacturing process conforms to the environmental regulations of the country of origin.

FSC www.fsc.org MIX Paper | Supporting responsible forestry FSC™ C110497

From the world of ISADORA MOON

MIRABELLE

and the Baby Dragons

Harriet Muncaster

OXFORD
UNIVERSITY PRESS

Chapter ONE

It was the start of half term, and I was in my bedroom polishing Violet's scales. Violet is my very special pet dragon and I *love* looking after her! Happy little puffs of smoke twirled out of her nose as I gently rubbed her with a soft cloth until her scales shimmered and shone.

'MIRABELLE!'

The door burst open, and my brother, Wilbur, barged into my bedroom, making Violet jump. A plume of purple fire shot out from her nostrils and scorched my duvet.

'Wilbur!' I sighed in exasperation. 'Look what you've done!'

Wilbur glanced at the scorch mark on the duvet.

'That's not *my* fault,' he said. 'It's Violet's!'

'It's *completely* your fault,' I said. '*You* shocked Violet!'

Big brothers can be *so* annoying sometimes.

'All right, I'm sorry,' replied Wilbur. 'But I *do* think Violet could do with some extra training.'

'She does *not* need extra training,' I huffed.

'Well, anyway,' Wilbur said, 'never mind that. I've come to tell you something exciting!'

'What?' I asked suspiciously.

'Mum just got a call on the crystal

ball from one of her friends, Gladys . . .'

'Gladys?' I said. 'You mean the witch who lives at the top of Stickle Mountain? The one who owns the dragon sanctuary?'

'Yes,' said Wilbur. 'And she's invited us to visit for half term. We're leaving tomorrow!'

'Really?' I gasped, completely forgetting my annoyance. 'Are you *sure*?'

'Yes!' cried Wilbur, jumping up and down with excitement. A couple of small rubber balls fell out of his pockets and bounced across the floor. Violet flew over to investigate. She loves playing with balls.

'Oops,' said Wilbur.

'What are those for?' I asked.

'Nothing really,' said Wilbur. He shrugged. 'Just practising the multiplying spell. We've been learning it at wizard school. I've got hundreds of bouncy balls now. I only started with three! Violet can keep those if she likes. Anyway, I'm off to pack my suitcase. You probably should pack yours too. A dragon sanctuary will be the perfect place for you to give Violet that extra training she needs.'

'Wilbur!' I leapt towards my brother, but he had already scooted out of the room, laughing.

'Only joking!' he yelled, running down the hallway. *'. . . Or was I?'*

Argh!

I closed the door and then turned towards Violet, scooping her up for a hug.

A whole week on Stickle Mountain at the dragon sanctuary!

That was a dream come true!

I had better start packing!

Chapter TWO

The following morning, I was woken *very* early by Dad poking his head around my bedroom door.

'It's time to go, Mirabelle!' he said. 'We're off to the dragon sanctuary. Bring your suitcase downstairs, please, and hop into the car.'

I gazed around my dark room,

blinking blearily.

'But it's still night-time!'

'I know,' said Dad. 'It's a long way to the dragon sanctuary. We've got to drive all the way to the mountains in the north.'

I swung my legs out of bed and stumbled sleepily over to my pile of clothes, pulling on my dress and tights. Then I dragged my suitcase down the stairs with a bump, bump, bump.

'There you are, Mirabelle!' said Mum, who was hurriedly gobbling down a slice of spider-sprinkled toast in the kitchen. 'Do you want some breakfast?'

'It's too early for breakfast,' I groaned.

'And *always* too early for spider-sprinkled toast,' added Wilbur, a disgusted look on his face. Wilbur and I didn't inherit Mum's love for witch food. We much prefer fairy food. Just like Dad!

'I've packed *us* a little fairy picnic for later,' said Dad as he grabbed my suitcase and dragged it outside. I followed him into the nippy night-time air and watched as he packed it carefully into the car. We don't use our car very often as Mum, Wilbur, and I have broomsticks, and Dad has fairy wings (which I have always been a bit jealous of!). Because of that, neither of my

parents are very good drivers. Mum goes far too fast, pressing her foot right down on the pedal and skidding around corners, while Dad does the opposite, crawling along at a snail's pace.

I wondered who would be driving today . . .

★ ★ ★

Three hours later, Dad, Wilbur, and I sat at a table outside a motorway stop, feeling frazzled. Dad's hair was sticking up on end from pulling on it so much, and Wilbur was cross because his wizard's hat had blown out of the window. Mum was calmly sipping her flask of chilli beetle tea.

'We've made *very* good progress,' she said happily. 'Almost halfway there.'

'That's because you've been driving like an absolute daredevil!' said Dad. 'It's not safe!'

'It's perfectly safe!' said Mum. 'I've put a spell on the car.'

'Well, even so,' said Dad, 'I think it would be best if *I* took over for the rest of the journey. It will save us all from getting whiplash!'

★ ★ ★

It was a nice change to have Dad driving at first. I could actually *see* what was going on outside the windows without it being a

blur. But the trail of hooting cars behind us *did* start to get a bit embarrassing. And it *did* mean that we arrived at the dragon sanctuary rather late. It was past dinner time when we crawled up the curvy mountain road, towards the house at the top with its pointy witch-hat turrets.

'Here we are at *last*!' said Mum pointedly.

As soon as Dad had parked the car, I jumped out, relieved to be able to stretch my legs finally. Violet swooped around my head, doing somersaults.

'Seraphina!' came a fruity-sounding voice from nearby. I turned to see Gladys, her arms outstretched, running towards my mum, followed by three dragons. She was short and stocky with a bob haircut and dressed in jodhpurs and welly boots with bits of hay stuck to them. 'It's so good to see you!' Gladys cried. 'And, oh my! How Wilbur and Mirabelle have grown!'

'It's so good to see you too!' Mum said, beaming. She gave her oldest friend a big hug as the dragons tumbled around at their feet. There was a beautiful pointy-nosed silver one, a little snub-nosed green one, and a teeny purple one that kept puffing lilac sparks. I couldn't stop staring. They were so cute!

'These ones are my *pets*,' Gladys explained. 'They're a domestic breed. They live in the house with me. I hope you don't mind scorch marks on the furniture. There are a lot of them in my house!'

'Not at *all*!' cried Mum. 'It adds character, I think.'

I knew that was an absolute lie! Mum *hates* scorch marks around *our* house. I was about to open my mouth to say so when Mum gave me a fierce look.

'Let's go inside, shall we?' said Gladys.

Gladys was right—there *were* a lot of scorch marks on the furniture. She may as well have decorated her house all in black and grey!

'It's lovely,' remarked Mum, gazing around. 'Very . . . monochrome.'

'Well, you have to put up with a *little* bit of wear and tear when you have so many dragons around the place,' said Gladys as she led us into the kitchen. 'Now, I did make some dinner for us all if you'd like some. Slug sausages and frogspawn mash! It's a bit cold now but . . .'

'Delicious!' exclaimed Mum.

Dad, Wilbur, and I stared at each other in horror.

'We had a fairy picnic in the car,' said Dad hurriedly. 'So, we, er . . . *vegetarians* don't need any dinner, thank you!'

'Oh, I forgot fairies were vegetarian,' said Gladys, looking a bit stricken. 'I *am* sorry!'

'Don't worry one bit, Gladys,' said Mum, patting her on the shoulder. 'All the more for us witches! I'm ravenous after a day in the car!'

Gladys immediately cheered up.

'Let's have a nice girly dinner together and catch up then!' she said. 'Mirabelle, Wilbur, Alvin, you're very welcome to pop out to have a look at the sanctuary if you like. Just don't go into any of the big outdoor enclosures because that's where the dragons who are nearly ready to go back to the wild are. They mustn't get used to spending too much time around people! You're welcome to go into the stables, though. That's where we keep the rescued dragons who used to be pets, plus any wild dragons who need extra care. Or otherwise, there's a TV in the sitting room . . .'

'Ooh!' said Wilbur. 'TV!'

'I think you've done enough sitting around today, Wilbur,' said Dad, steering him towards the back door. 'Let's all go and stretch our legs. A little walk to the stables would be lovely! Thank you, Gladys.'

Chapter THREE

It was dark outside, and hundreds of tiny pinprick stars twinkled in the dusky sky. We were so high up on Stickle Mountain that I could see for miles and miles and miles! We could also see some of the outdoor dragon enclosures just below. They were huge open spaces with mesh roofs so that the dragons couldn't fly away before they were ready. Some of the enclosures had lots of fir trees and bushes inside them. Some were full of craggy caves, glinting with crystals, and some had been magicked to be full of permanently swirling snow and ice.

The stables were in a long, low building near the house. Golden light peeped through the cracks in the door as we approached. Inside, there were lots of different pens full of sweet-smelling hay. Each pen had a trough of charcoal for the dragons to eat.

There were ALL kinds of different dragons here! Star-spotted ones and stripy ones, shiny metallic glimmery shimmery ones, and even some leathery feathery ones!

'Ooooh!' I said, gazing around in wonder.

Wilbur sneezed. Hay always makes his nose tickly.

'Golly!' said Dad, stepping back as a rather large dragon stood up in its pen and began to stretch its neck towards us, flapping its huge wings so that a breeze blew all around, swirling strands of hay into the air.

'Down, Cuthbert!' came a voice, and a young witch who looked only a little bit older than me stepped out from behind the dragon. She had fiery red curly hair and a spray of freckles across her nose. She didn't look too pleased to see us.

I watched in amazement as Cuthbert settled down again in his pen, blowing a spiral of smoke out from his nostrils.

The witch stared suspiciously at me, Wilbur, and Dad.

'Who are you?' she asked.

'We're friends of Gladys,' said Dad, holding out his hand for her to shake. 'What's your name?'

'Ember,' said the witch. 'I work here.'

'You *work* here?' I gasped, thinking about how Ember must have the most amazing job in the *world*! 'Oh wow! Can I help you? I love dragons! I know everything about them! I have a pet dragon, you know. Violet! Here she is, look!'

I plucked Violet off my shoulder and held her out for Ember to inspect. Violet wriggled crossly, sliding out of my grasp and fluttering up into the air. She does not like to be handled too much.

Ember raised an eyebrow and smirked.

'I don't need any help, thanks,' she said. 'I think you'd just get in my way.'

'What?!' I cried indignantly. 'I won't *get in your way*! I think you'd find me *super* helpful. As I said, I know everything about dragons.'

'Except training them,' muttered Wilbur under his breath.

I gave him a sharp jab with my elbow.

'I think it sounds like a great idea for you to help out, Mirabelle!' said Dad. 'If Gladys agrees. I'm sure Ember will be able to give you some great tips. *Tomorrow.*'

'I don't need *tips*,' I said through

gritted teeth. 'I know what I'm doing!'

Ember didn't reply, but she looked annoyed.

'I want to help too, if Mirabelle's helping!' piped up Wilbur.

'Well, I'm sure Ember would be glad to have you *both* helping,' said Dad, smiling obliviously.

Ember scowled.

I scowled, too, just as Mum's voice floated through the stable doors.

'Mirabelle? Wilbur? It's time to get ready for bed!'

Chapter FOUR

The following morning, with Violet still snoozing in bed, Wilbur and I got up bright and early, ready to help out at the stables. Gladys had said that she would be *delighted* for us to 'muck in'.

'I had better show you which draglings I'd like you to look after,' she said, putting on a pair of purple welly boots and stomping out of the house. 'Come with me!'

Wilbur and I followed Gladys into the fresh early morning air and towards the stables. She pushed open the double doors, and we stepped inside. Immediately, there was a skittering and rustling as all the dragons got up to see who had come in.

'It's me, my *darlings*!' cried Gladys and she began to walk up and down, petting as many of the dragons as she could. They flapped their wings excitedly and puffed glittery grey smoke from their nostrils.

'Doesn't the hay ever catch fire?' asked Wilbur.

'Oh no!' said Gladys. 'It's got a special fire-resistant spell on it. Very important!'

She stopped by the pen of a particularly sweet, small dragon with tiny stars on its wings.

'This is Penelope,' she said. 'Penelope only came into the sanctuary last week. She'd been abandoned by her owner. It's very sad. I'm hoping someone will come along and adopt her soon.'

‘Oh, she’s so cute!’ I squealed, giving Penelope a little stroke on her nose.

We passed the big dragon who we had seen last night.

‘Cuthbert!’ said Gladys. ‘He’s been at the sanctuary for a while. He’s full-grown, as you can see!’

‘Why is he here?’ I asked.

‘The poor thing was injured,’ explained Gladys. ‘He’s better now, but we need to make sure that he’s strong enough to move into the outdoor enclosures. Although . . .’ she gave Cuthbert a pat on his large scaly back, ‘I think he quite likes it here!’

Cuthbert closed his eyes and snorted

happily just as the stable doors opened, and Ember walked in carrying two buckets of charcoal.

'Ember!' said Gladys. 'This is Mirabelle and Wilbur.'

'Yes,' said Ember without smiling. 'We met last night.'

'Oh, wonderful!' exclaimed Gladys. 'So, you're already friends! Well, you'll be pleased to hear that Mirabelle and Wilbur are going to help you out at the sanctuary this morning!'

Ember did *not* look pleased.

'I thought you could give them some tips,' continued Gladys, 'seeing as you have such a wonderful way with dragons.'

Ember just nodded unenthusiastically and turned away to feed some dragons in the pen furthest away from us.

'Marvellous!' said Gladys. 'Ember really is such a wonderful worker, Mirabelle and Wilbur. So knowledgeable! I'm lucky to have her here. She'll be able to teach you both so much.'

I forced myself to smile and nod at Gladys.

But really, I had no intention of letting Ember teach me anything. I didn't need help! I was sure that I already knew everything there was to know about looking after dragons.

Gladys glanced at her watch.

'I had better get back to the house,' she said. 'It's almost breakfast time, and I planned to cook a big witch fry-up for your mum and me. I've bought crocodile eggs in specially! But first, let me show you the draglings I'd like you to take care of . . .'

She beckoned for us to follow her to

the end of the stables, where there was one big pen that Wilbur and I hadn't had a chance to look in yet.

'Ooh!' I squealed.

Inside the pen, snuggled up peacefully in a pile of hay, was a clutch of the tiniest baby dragons I had ever seen! They looked small enough to curl up in the palm of my hand.

'They only came in yesterday,' whispered Gladys. 'I found them abandoned on a cold mountain crag. I waited for hours to see if the mother would come back for them, but she seemed to have disappeared. It's terribly sad. Anyway, they're only very little, so they shouldn't be much bother to look after. I'm sure you and Wilbur can manage to keep an eye on them today.'

'Definitely!' I said, hopping up and down with excitement. 'Don't worry, Gladys. I'm practically an expert in dragons.'

‘Me too!’ butted in Wilbur.

‘Splendid!’ said Gladys. ‘Of course, they will get a bit friskier once they wake up.’

‘Uh huh!’ I said, nodding my head but not really listening. ‘They’ll be safe with us, Gladys. You’ll see!’

‘OK then!’ said Gladys, smiling. ‘Well, I’ll leave you to it. And don’t forget, you can always ask Ember to help if you’re not sure what to do.’

‘Oh, we know what to do,’ I replied confidently.

Chapter FIVE

Once Gladys had gone, I leant over the pen and just stared at the jewel-coloured baby dragons. They were absolutely *adorable*! The purple one was gently snoring, sending lilac sparks out from its nostrils.

'What are their names?' asked Wilbur, peering at a clipboard attached to the pen. 'Ruby, Amber, Citrine, Emerald, Sapphire, and Amethyst!'

A rainbow of jewels!

'How perfect!' I exclaimed.

The little red dragling—Ruby—began to stir, opening her eyes slightly. When she saw Wilbur and me staring down at her, she hopped up and stretched, flapping her tiny wings.

'Are you hungry, Ruby?' I asked, poking my finger through the bars so that she could sniff it. 'Wilbur, you'd better go and fetch some charcoal for them.'

'Me?' said Wilbur. 'No, I'll wait with the draglings. *You* can go and fetch the charcoal.'

I couldn't be bothered to argue.

'Fine!' I said.

I hurried back past all the other pens, patting the other dragons as I went. I passed Ember on her way back into the stables carrying another two buckets of charcoal. It occurred to me that I didn't know where the charcoal was kept, but I didn't want to ask her *anything*! How hard could it be to find?

I stepped outside and gazed around. Right next to the stables, there was a large shed. There were lumps of charcoal scattered outside the door.

That must be it!

Triumphantly, I pushed open the door to the shed and peered through it. Inside, there was a giant mound of charcoal. Perfect! I grabbed a bucket and took a large scoop. It was heavy! Then I lugged it back into the stables, passing Ember as I went. She gave me a strange look.

'What are you doing?' she asked.

'What do you mean?' I said. 'The baby dragons need breakfast, of course!'

Ember smirked.

'Teeny newborn dragons don't eat huge lumps of charcoal,' she said. 'Everyone knows that! You have to powder it for them.'

'Oh,' I said, feeling my face flush. 'Yes,

I knew that. I just haven't got around to crushing it yet.'

'Well, the charcoal crusher is *outside*,' said Ember, pointedly. 'Round the back.'

'Right,' I said.

I turned quickly and hurried back out of the stables, my cheeks burning. I found the funny-looking machine and stood staring at it in confusion for a while.

How was I supposed to work *that*?

It was shaped like a witch's hat and had a twirly whirly slide spiralling down towards the brim. I did not want to go back inside and ask Ember *anything*, so I spent a while experimenting.

Eventually, I worked out that the charcoal was supposed to whizz down the slide and disappear through a little hole. There was a loud *CRUNCH,* then black powder sprinkled out beneath the brim of the hat and into a bucket. Once I got going it was a lot of fun, and I got so absorbed that I forgot all about Ember and my embarrassing mistake.

'You took *ages,* Mirabelle!' said Wilbur when I finally returned with a whole bucket of twinkling crushed charcoal for the draglings.

'I know,' I said. 'I had to crush the charcoal, of course! Everyone knows that baby draglings this small need to have it powdered.'

'Oh, uh yeah, I knew that,' said Wilbur, going a tiny bit pink.

All the draglings were awake now and fluttering around the pen, their scales shimmering in the light. I slipped into the pen. When the babies noticed me with the powdered charcoal, they came flying over, clustering around the bucket to try and stick their noses into it.

'Hang on!' I giggled, bending down to try and pour some of the charcoal into a little trough. 'Wait for it to be *served*!'

But the draglings didn't want to wait to be served. They squeaked and fluttered and flapped so excitedly, dive-bombing into the bucket so that clouds of charcoal puffed out into the air and onto everything nearby, including my face and my clothes.

'Uh oh!' said Wilbur, who had stepped back a few paces outside the pen.

'It will brush off!' I said, putting the bucket down—much to the draglings' delight—and wiping at my clothes. But my hands were covered in charcoal, too, and it just ended up making more mess. Out of the corner of my eye, I could see Ember staring at me in an amused sort of way from a pen nearby. I gritted my teeth.

'Oh!' said Wilbur, suddenly, pointing to a little tube. 'I meant to say that I think you were supposed to pour the charcoal down this thing, Mirabelle. It goes straight into the trough from outside the pen.'

'Well, it's a bit late now!' I said a little snappily. 'You could have mentioned that earlier.'

'I forgot!' said Wilbur.

When the draglings had finished eating, they began to zoom around their pen, spinning and somersaulting, blowing out little plumes of multicoloured fire. They had so much energy, and they seemed very interested in me! They kept sniffing at my hair and landing on my head and shoulders with their little clawed feet. The blue one—Sapphire—blew out a snort of excited sparks.

‘Woah!’ cried Wilbur suddenly. ‘Watch out, Mirabelle!’

A tiny spark had landed on my hair, which was smoking slightly. There was a horrible frizzly smell. Wilbur leapt into the pen and began to bat at my hair with his hands, whacking me much harder than necessary in the panic. The draglings all shot away into the corners of the pen, cowering beneath their wings.

'All right, Wilbur!' I yelled. 'That's enough. You're frightening the draglings.'

'Your hair was about to catch fire!' he said.

'It was only smoking a tiny bit,' I said, examining the tip of a frizzled strand of hair.

Hmm.

'Is everything all right?' asked Ember, hurrying over. 'Do you need help? Newborn dragons can be quite a handful, you know. They've got a lot to learn!'

'I know!' I replied, pasting a smile onto my face. 'But we're fine, thank you, Ember. Wilbur and I have everything under control. We don't need your help.'

Ember didn't look convinced. But she just shrugged and went back to the pen she had been in before. I craned my neck to see what she was doing. She had a crate of balls and soft toys with her. The little draglings she was playing with looked calm and happy. None of them were blowing out sparks that were in danger of setting her on fire. I hated to admit it to myself, but she really did seem to have a special way with them.

'We should *play* with our baby dragons!' I hissed to Wilbur. 'Where are your bouncy balls? They would be the perfect size!'

'I didn't bring them,' said Wilbur. 'I couldn't find them when I woke up yesterday morning.'

I looked around, wondering where the toys for the draglings were kept. I did *not* want to ask Ember, but I couldn't see another crate of toys anywhere. I did spot a wheelbarrow and a couple of forks standing nearby, though.

'I think we should clean out the draglings' pen instead,' I said to Wilbur.

'OK,' he said and shrugged.

I pushed the wheelbarrow into the pen, and Wilbur and I began to shovel old hay into it.

'Atishoo!' said Wilbur.

The six teeny draglings seemed very interested in what we were doing. They fluttered back towards us, still blowing out sparks. I stepped back a few paces. I felt a little more wary of them now—I didn't want my hair to catch fire again.

'NO!' I said firmly, wagging my finger at them because that's what I do with Violet when she gets overexcited.

But the tiny newborn draglings didn't listen. They were so small and young—they probably just didn't understand. They kept flapping around my head, poking me with their noses and squeaking. Then they started to dive-bomb into the pile of hay in the wheelbarrow so that strands of it flew out everywhere!

I decided I would just have to try and ignore them.

'You'll have to mind the draglings while I go and find some more hay bales,' I said to Wilbur when the wheelbarrow was finally full. I pushed it out of the stables and into the fresh air, where I bumped straight into Gladys, who seemed to be in a hurry.

'Mirabelle!' she said. 'Can't stop! I've just been called up into the mountains to see to a dragon with an injured wing! Are you looking for more hay bales? They're in the barn down the track, behind the house. The rubbish heap is there, too.'

'Oh!' I replied, gratefully. 'Thank you!'

I hurried away from Gladys, pushing the wheelbarrow past the house and onto a track.

A very long track.

I hadn't realized the barn would be quite so far away!

But at least it was downhill.

I pushed the wheelbarrow along, humming to myself. I was going to do a *super* fantastic job of cleaning out the draglings' pen! Gladys was going to be so pleased! And Ember would be able to see how knowledgeable I was about baby dragons.

When I got to the barn, I tipped all the old hay out of the wheelbarrow onto a big heap outside the door and then went inside to get some more hay bales. There they were! Stacked up and golden and slightly twinkling from the fire-resistant magic. I reached out to lift one and . . .

'OOF!'

It was much heavier than I had expected!

I pushed and heaved and panted and eventually managed to slide *one* of the hay bales into my wheelbarrow. It only just fitted!

Wiping my forehead, I turned away from the barn and began to push the wheelbarrow back along the track.

It was much, *much* harder this time. The hay was heavy, and I was going uphill all the way! By the time I got back to the stables and pushed the wheelbarrow into the pen, I was out of breath and sweating all over. Wilbur didn't look much better. His hair was all tousled, and there was a scorch mark on his sleeve.

'What's happened to you?' he asked,

staring at my red face. 'You took ages! It's been a nightmare looking after the draglings on my own!'

'The barn is so far away! And it's all uphill on the way back,' I complained, flopping down in the pen for a few moments' rest. Immediately, the draglings swarmed over to me. Ruby puffed red sparks from her nostrils, narrowly missing my skirt, so I jumped right back up again.

'It's definitely your turn. Go and get the next hay bale!' I said to Wilbur. 'One hay bale won't be enough to make it comfortable in here.'

'Do I *have* to?' he asked. 'I'm *exhausted*!'

'Yes!' I insisted.

Wilbur frowned reluctantly. Then he got a little bit of a shifty look in his eye.

'I have a better idea!' he whispered. 'Why don't I use my new multiplying spell to make more hay bales? Then *neither* of us has to go back to the barn. Ember won't notice!'

I looked across the stables. Ember was now in one of the far pens by the door, preoccupied with polishing Penelope's scales. The dragon was making happy purring sounds.

'I suppose it *would* be better for us both to stay with the draglings,' I said. 'They *are* quite a handful.'

'Exactly!' said Wilbur. 'And the spell will only take a moment. I'll just magic up a few more hay bales. We can make it so nice and comfortable in here for the draglings!'

'OK,' I said, starting to feel excited. 'Let's do it!'

We both glanced back at Ember to check that she wasn't watching; then Wilbur began to wiggle his fingers in a wizardy sort of way.

'Riddly diddly duplio ponk!' he hissed, and I tried not to laugh.

Personally, I always think wizard magic looks a little bit silly.

Little purple sparks began to fizzle at Wilbur's fingertips and fly off towards the hay bale.

'Riddly tiddly duplio—

ATISHOO!'

Suddenly, Wilbur gave an almighty sneeze! The sparks from his fingertips shot off in a completely different direction, away from the hay bale and towards the six baby draglings in the pen.

'Wilbur!' I gasped in horror as a flurry of jewel-coloured sparks began to swirl around the baby draglings. When the sparks cleared, I could see that all of them had been duplicated! There were now two Rubies, two Ambers, two Citrines, two Emeralds, two Sapphires, and two Amethysts! It was impossible to tell which draglings were the original ones and which ones were magicked up!

The draglings all seemed extremely excited to see each other. They began rolling about and playing, zooming around their pen and squeaking. They were *so* excitable that they wouldn't stop blowing out sparks, and Wilbur and I had to swiftly leave the pen to stop our clothes from sizzling.

'Oh no!' I wailed.

'Whoops,' said Wilbur.

Chapter SIX

'It's more than a "whoops" Wilbur!' I cried—but not too loud because I didn't want Ember to notice what was going on.

'Sorry,' said Wilbur, looking a bit shamefaced. 'It's this hay; it just makes my nose so tickly!'

We both stared at the *twelve* baby dragons in the pen.

'What are we going to do?' I whispered.

'I don't know,' said Wilbur. 'But they'll probably calm down eventually. They can't come to any harm in the pen! I'm sure they'll fall asleep again soon.'

'What will they sleep on though?' I asked. 'There's definitely not enough hay in there for all twelve of them!'

'Shall I try the spell again?' said Wilbur as he rolled up his sleeves. 'I promise I won't sneeze this time.'

'NO!' I hissed firmly. 'I think one of us had better go and fetch the hay the normal non-magic way.'

The draglings were going berserk!

Surely, Ember was going to notice what was going on soon. Fetching more hay suddenly felt like the better option.

I think Wilbur must have been thinking the same because he suddenly grabbed the wheelbarrow and zoomed off with it.

'I'll go,' he called over his shoulder. 'It's time I did something useful. Back soon, Mirabelle!'

I stared in dismay at the pen of baby draglings, wishing that I hadn't been left on my own with them. One of the Emeralds was trying to wriggle through the mesh ceiling of the pen, craning its neck towards me and puffing out green sparks.

I took a step backwards.

Toys! That was what the draglings needed! I had to find some toys to distract them! But where were they kept? I didn't want to have to ask Ember.

But what other choice did I have?

I hurried along towards Penelope's pen.

'Uh, Ember,' I said. 'I just have *one* question.'

'Hey,' said Ember, turning around. She sounded a bit less unfriendly than before. Maybe she could sense my desperation.

'Are you OK?' she asked. 'Do you need help?'

I was about to shake my head. *All* I needed to know was where the toys were kept. But before I could stop myself, I started to nod instead.

'Wilbur and I have made a mistake,' I said. 'He tried to do a multiplying spell to duplicate the hay so that we didn't have to walk all the way to the barn, but he accidentally duplicated all the dragons! Now there are twelve of them and they won't calm down! They need some toys, but I don't know where the toys are, and there's not enough hay in their pen either . . .'

I trailed off, and Ember blinked at me, a slightly amused look on her face.

'I did think things didn't sound quite right,' she said.

'We need help!' I admitted. 'Please, Ember! I thought I knew everything about baby dragons, but it turns out there's still so much to learn! I just don't know what to do with them. They're so energetic! Not like my pet dragon Violet at all!'

Ember laughed.

'Well, to be fair, you *are* looking after a particularly boisterous breed of *wild* dragon,' she said. 'But I have a few tricks to help calm them.'

'You do?' I cried in relief. 'Teach me, please!'

Ember knelt in front of the draglings' pen. She started to make a funny ticking sound with her tongue. At once, the

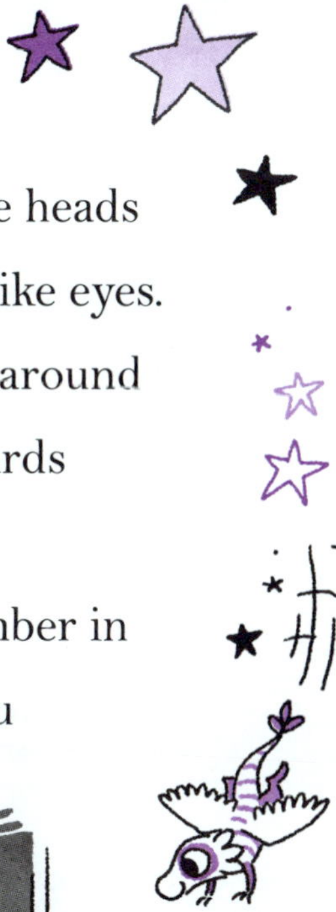

draglings began to turn their little heads towards her, blinking their jewel-like eyes. The ones who had been whizzing around in the air began to flap down towards the ground.

'Good draglings,' soothed Ember in a calm, gentle voice. 'Let's find you some toys.'

She got up and hurried away. The draglings started to get fidgety again, so I tried to make the same clicking sound with my tongue. I didn't manage to do it quite as well as Ember, but the draglings still seemed to like it.

A few moments later, Ember reappeared with a box of toys. There were balls and tugs and chews inside it.

'This will stop them blowing out sparks all the time,' she said, setting the box on the ground. Together we took the toys out one by one and began to slip them through the door of the pen. The draglings took the toys and began to play, biting and rolling and flapping. They seemed happy but much less manic now. And most importantly, none of them were blowing sparks at us! Everything felt so much more under control now that Ember was helping me. She really did have the magic touch! I wished I had just asked for her help earlier on instead of thinking that I knew better.

Just then, the door opened, and Wilbur came bustling through, pushing the wheelbarrow. His face was bright red, and he looked very out of breath. He stopped and stared when he saw Ember sitting next to me by the draglings' pen.

'Ember's just teaching me some tricks!' I said. 'I told her about the multiplying spell.'

'That was my fault,' said Wilbur, sounding embarrassed.

'It's OK,' replied Ember. 'I love dragons so much! So *I* don't mind! And anyway, the magicked-up ones will disappear soon. Duplicated things never last long—everyone knows that!'

'Yeah,' said Wilbur unconvincingly. 'Of *course* I knew that.'

Together the three of us heaved the hay bale off the wheelbarrow and into the pen. Ember began to pull great handfuls of hay, patting them down to make nice squashy beds for the draglings.

'You didn't actually need to clean out their pen today, by the way,' she said. 'Gladys and I usually clean out all the pens on a Tuesday and a Friday!'

'*All* of them!' gasped Wilbur, staring at the wheelbarrow and looking exhausted.

'Gladys has a tractor,' said Ember. 'We put all the hay bales on that! Much easier than using the wheelbarrow. It's all uphill on the way back from the barn, you know.'

'*We know,*' Wilbur and I both said together.

Soon the draglings' pen looked all nice and cosy. Some of the draglings had got tired of playing and were snuggling down for a little sleep.

'Aren't they sweet?' said Ember. 'Now that they're not being little terrors!'

'So sweet,' I agreed. 'Thank you, Ember, for all your help. I'm sorry I didn't ask you before. I really did think I knew how to do everything myself.'

'I'm sorry I was rude before,' said Ember. 'I just find it hard to talk to people sometimes. I prefer dragons!'

We all laughed.

'Anyway,' said Ember. 'It's time for lunch! 'Shall we go back to the house?'

Chapter SEVEN

'How did you get on in the stables?' asked Gladys once we were all sitting down at the table. Mum, Gladys, and Ember were all having spider sandwiches, but Dad had thankfully magicked up some cheese and pickle toasties for Wilbur and me.

'It was . . . interesting,' said Wilbur as he munched his toastie.

'We learnt a lot from Ember,' I said. 'And I want her to teach me *more*!'

'I'd love Mirabelle's help,' Ember said, beaming.

None of us mentioned the duplicated draglings.

'Well, I have some good news!' said Gladys. 'The draglings' mother has been found! She'd torn her wing and couldn't fly back to her nest, but I've patched it up this morning and brought her to one of the outdoor enclosures. We'll take her babies back to her after lunch!'

I felt nervous about what Gladys would say when she saw the extra draglings, but when we arrived back at their pen they had already disappeared.

'Told you they wouldn't last long!' whispered Ember.

I watched as Gladys and Ember opened the door of the pen and slipped inside, beckoning for me to follow. Together we coaxed the draglings into a carry box, using a special finger click that Ember showed me. Then we walked up a steep little mountain path to a large outdoor enclosure that contained lots of trees and a craggy-looking cave.

'The mother dragon is in here,' said Gladys. 'I've named her Opal. You'll see why!'

Cautiously, I followed Gladys and Ember into the cave. Curled up on a bed of straw was the most beautiful dragon I had ever seen! Her scales glimmered and shimmered every colour of the rainbow. Just like an opal!

'Ooh!' whispered Wilbur.

'She's so pretty!' I gasped.

Opal seemed wary at first, but when she realized we had her babies in the carry box she jumped up, making a sort of crying noise. The babies all poked their long snouts out through the bars and squeaked too. Hurriedly, Gladys put the carry box down and opened the door. The little babies tumbled out, skittering along the ground and flapping their wings to get to their mother as fast as they could. I felt my eyes well up with tears as I watched the little dragons reunite with their mother, climbing all over her and snuggling in beneath her injured wing.

'Warms the heart, doesn't it?' said

Gladys, smiling. 'Those babies will be much better off with their mother to show them the way now, but you did a great job looking after them in the meantime, Mirabelle and Wilbur. Thank you!'

I knew that wasn't strictly true. Wilbur and I hadn't done it on our own. Just like the baby dragons who needed guidance from their mother, we needed guidance from someone who knew better than us too.

'Ember helped a lot,' I admitted.

'Well, you all did a wonderful job,' said Gladys. 'The babies seem very happy!'

And she was right. The draglings were *delighted* to be back where they belonged. Opal was overjoyed too. She kept blowing glittering plumes of rainbow smoke up into the air, and I knew she was smiling, smiling, smiling.

Turn the page
for some
mischievous
things to make
and do!

How to make your own dragon mask

Turn yourself into a dragon with this fun dragon mask!

What you will need:

- Paper plate
- Paint (what colour dragon would you like to be?!)
- Paintbrushes
- Scissors
- Glue
- Construction paper (green, red, yellow, or any other colours you'd like for decoration)
- Felt-tip pens or crayons
- Elastic band or string
- A grown-up assistant to help you

Method

1. Prepare your work area by laying down some newspapers or an old tablecloth to protect the surface.

2. Use a paintbrush to coat the entire surface of the plate with the paint.

3. Let it dry completely.

4. Ask your grown-up assistant to carefully cut out eye holes near the top of the paper plate. Make sure they are large enough to see through comfortably.

5. Using the construction paper cut out dragon features such as horns, spikes, and teeth. Glue them onto the paper plate to create the dragon's face.

6. Use felt-tip pens or crayons to add details like scales, nostrils, and any other decorations you'd like.

7. Ask your grown-up assistant to help you attach an elastic band or string to the sides of the mask. Make sure it's comfortable!

8. You're now ready to be a dragon! Have fun roaring, stomping, and flying around!

9. Remember to help tidy up afterwards!

How to make dragon-scale biscuits

Mirabelle and Wilbur would love to eat these delicious dragon-scale biscuits!

Ingredients

For biscuits:

- 275g plain flour
- 100g unsalted butter, softened at room temperature
- 100g caster sugar
- 1 free-range egg, lightly beaten
- 1 tsp vanilla extract
- Food colouring (green, red, yellow, or any colours you prefer)

Equipment:

- Baking tray
- Greaseproof paper
- Mixing bowl
- Wooden spoon
- Fork
- Sieve
- Rolling pin
- Cookie cutters
- Wire rack
- Knife
- A grown-up assistant to help

Method

1. Preheat your oven to 175°C/350°F.

2. Line a baking sheet with greaseproof paper.

3. In a mixing bowl, use the wooden spoon to mix together the butter and sugar until smooth and creamy.

4. Add the egg and vanilla extract, and mix until well combined.

5. Sift in the flour and stir until the mixture comes together as a dough. You may need to use your hands to knead the dough gently until it comes together.

6. Divide the dough into several portions, depending on how many colours of dragon scales you'd like to create. You can start with two or three portions for variety.

7. Add a few drops of food colouring to each portion of dough and knead until the colour is evenly distributed. Have fun mixing the colours to create vibrant dragon scales. Remember: a little bit of food colouring goes a long way!

8. Lightly flour your clean working surface to prevent sticking.

9. Roll out each coloured portion of dough into a thin sheet, about 1/4 inch thick, using a rolling pin.

10. Use cookie cutters to cut out shapes from the rolled-out dough. You can use any shape you like, but triangles work well to look like dragon scales!

11. Once you've cut out the biscuits, it's time to create the dragon scales! Use the back of a butter knife or a fork to gently press scales onto the surface of each biscuit. Experiment with different patterns and designs.

12. Ask your grown-up assistant to place the biscuits onto the prepared baking sheet and bake in the preheated oven for 10-12 minutes, or until the edges are lightly golden brown.

13. Ask your grown-up assistant to remove the baking tray from the oven and place the biscuits on a wire rack to cool.

14. Once cooled, enjoy these delicious dragon-scale biscuits together as a tasty treat!

How to make a handprint dragon!

What you will need:

- Washable paint in colours of your choice
- Paintbrushes
- Paper
- Felt-tips or crayons
- Scissors
- Water and kitchen roll/a towel to clean your hands afterwards!
- A grown-up assistant to help

Method

1. Prepare your work area by laying down some newspapers or an old tablecloth to protect the surface.

2. Paint the palm of one hand with your chosen colour—this will be your dragon's body, legs, and tail.

3. Carefully press your painted hand onto the paper. Make sure that your fingers are spread apart slightly to create space for the dragon's legs and tail. Press firmly but gently to ensure a clear handprint.

4. Repeat for as many dragons as you would like!

5. Wash your hands.

6. Leave your handprints to dry completely.

7. Using the crayons or felt-tips give your dragon a head!

8. Add some detail to your dragon. You could add horns, spikes, scales, and anything else you can think of!

9. Cut your dragon out, and display it proudly!

10. If you like you can get even more creative—why not give your dragon a name, create a background to stick your dragon on, or maybe write a story about it.

Spot the difference!

Can you find **five** differences between these two pictures of Ember and the draglings?

Answers

Ember's eyebrows are missing, the stripes on one leg of her tights are missing, the star on her apron is missing, the end of the white dragling's tail has changed colour, the purple dragling is missing its white patterns.

Matching draglings!

Can you find the two draglings that are the same?

Answer

The two white draglings with purple legs and purple and white stripy tails—top left of the left-hand page, and bottom right of this page.

Quiz

What kind of job should you do with dragons? Take the quiz to find out!

1. What's your favourite thing about dragons?

A. Their intelligence

B. Their magical powers and abilities

C. Their beautiful scales

2. If you found a sick dragon, what would you do?

A. Try to nurse it back to health myself

B. Take it to a dragon sanctuary where experts can help

C. Call somebody who could come and help it

3. What do you think is the best way to learn about dragons?

A. Reading books about them and studying them

B. Going on adventures to see dragons in the wild

C. Listening to stories from experienced dragon experts

Results

Mostly As

You should be a dragon vet! Your love of learning and caring nature make you the perfect dragon healer.

Mostly Bs

You should take care of dragon habitats! With your love of adventure and respect for the wild, you'd be brilliant at keeping them safe in their natural habitat.

Mostly Cs

You should perhaps not work with dragons but admire them from a distance! Your appreciation for dragons' beauty and understanding of their wild nature mean you're happiest watching them from afar.

To visit Harriet Muncaster's
website, go to
harrietmuncaster.co.uk

From the world of
ISADORA MOON
MIRABELLE
Gets up to Mischief

From the world of
ISADORA MOON
MIRABELLE
Has a Bad Day
Half witch, half fairy, totally naughty!
Harriet Muncaster

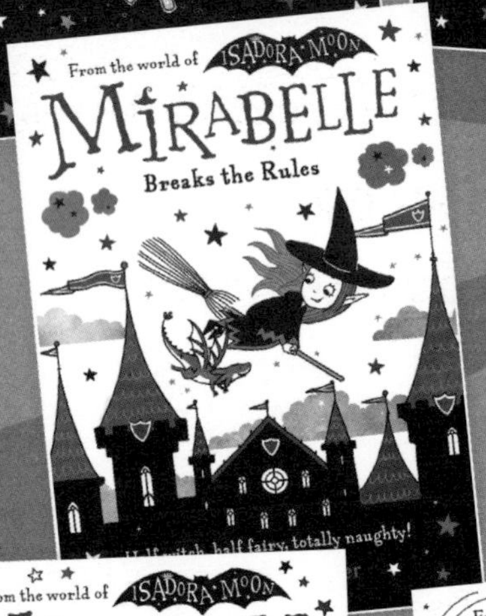
From the world of
ISADORA MOON
MIRABELLE
Breaks the Rules

From the world of
ISADORA MOON
MIRABELLE
in Double Trouble

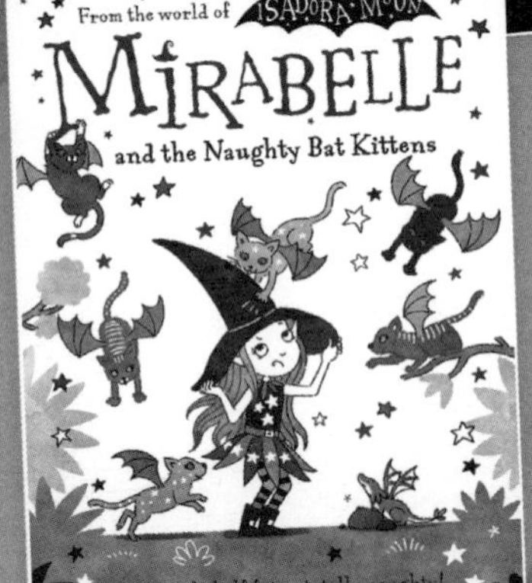
From the world of
ISADORA MOON
MIRABELLE
and the Naughty Bat Kittens
Half witch, half fairy, totally naughty!
Harriet Muncaster

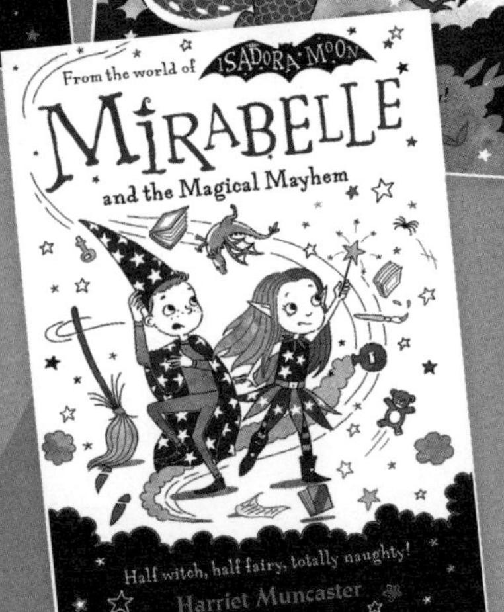
From the world of
ISADORA MOON
MIRABELLE
and the Magical Mayhem
Half witch, half fairy, totally naughty!
Harriet Muncaster

From the world of ISADORA MOON
MIRABELLE
Takes Charge
Harriet Muncaster
From the world of ISADORA MOON
MIRABELLE
Wants to Win
From the world of ISADORA MOON
MIRABELLE
and the Haunted House
From the world of ISADORA MOON
MIRABELLE
and the Midnight Feast
Half witch, half fairy, totally naughty!
Harriet Muncaster
From the world of ISADORA MOON
MIRABELLE
and the Picnic Pranks
Half witch, half fairy, totally naughty!
Harriet Muncaster

ISADORA MOON

ISADORA MOON
Goes on a School Trip
Half vampire, half fairy,
Harriet Mun

ISADORA MOON
Has a Sleepover
f fairy, totally unique!
Muncaster

ISADORA MOON
Goes to the Fair
vampire, half fairy, totally unique!
Harriet Muncas

ISADORA MOON
Makes Winter Magic
Half vampire, half fairy, totally unique!
Harriet Muncaster

ISADORA MOON
Goes on Holiday
Half vampire, half fairy, totally unique!
Harriet Muncaster

ISADORA MOON
Puts on a Show
Half vampire, half fairy,
Harriet

ISADORA MOON
Under the Sea
half fairy, totally unique!
Muncaster

ISADORA MOON
Goes to a Wedding
half fairy, totally

ISADORA MOON
Meets the Tooth Fairy
Half vampire, half fairy, totally unique!
Harriet Muncaster

ISADORA MOON
and the Shooting Star
Half vampire, half fairy, totally unique!
Harriet Muncaster

ISADORA MOON
Gets the Magic Pox
Half vampire, half fairy,
Harriet

ISADORA MOON
and the New Girl
fairy, totally unique!
Muncaster

ISADORA MOON
and the Frost Festival
Harriet

ISADORA MOON
Helps Out
Half vampire, half fairy, totally unique!
Harriet Muncaster

ISADORA MOON
Makes a Wish
Plus Isadorable activities!
Half vampire, half fairy, totally unique!
Harriet Muncaster

Get ready to meet
Isadora's mermaid
friend, Emerald!

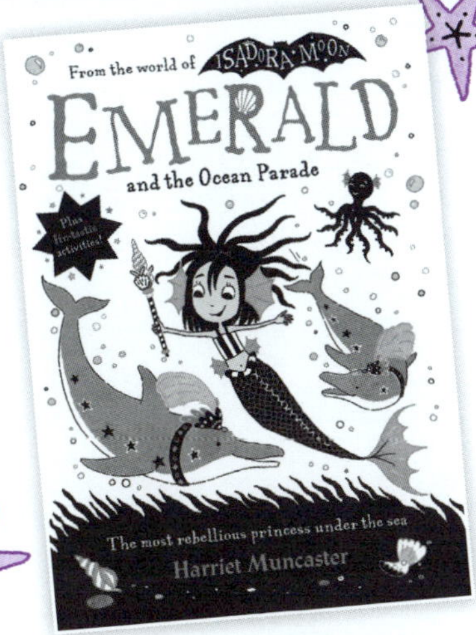
From the world of
ISADORA MOON
EMERALD
and the Ocean Parade
The most rebellious princess under the sea
Harriet Muncaster

From the world of
ISADORA MOON
EMERALD
and the Sea Sprites
The most rebellious princess under the sea
Harriet Muncaster

From the world of
ISADORA MOON
EMERALD
and the Lost Treasure
The most rebellious princess under the sea
Harriet Muncaster

From the world of
ISADORA MOON
EMERALD
and the Runaway Royal
The most rebellious princess under the sea
Harriet Muncaster

Harriet Muncaster

Harriet Muncaster, that's me! I'm the creator of three young fiction series, Isadora Moon, Mirabelle, and Emerald, as well as the Victoria Stitch series for older readers. I love anything teeny tiny, anything starry, and everything glittery.

Like Mirabelle?
Why not try . . .

KENNETH GRAHAME
ILLUSTRATED BY DAVID ROBERTS
THE WIND IN THE WILLOWS

CROAKY
SEARCH FOR THE SASQUATCH
MATTY LONG
FROM THE CREATOR OF
SUPER HAPPY MAGIC FOREST

Kitty
and the
Snowball Bandit
Girl by day. Cat by night. Ready for adventure.
Written by Paula Harrison • Illustrated by Jenny Løvlie

GÒRDÓN
THE MEANEST GOOSE ON EARTH
Alex Latimer